USBORNE EASY READING

The Runaway Orange

Felicity Brooks

Models by Jo Litchfield 🌼 Designed by Non Figg

Language consultant: Dr. Marlynne Grant BSc, CertEd, MEdPsych, PhD, AFBPs, CPsychol

Photography by Howard Allman 🌼 Edited by Jenny Tyler

This story is about Polly and Jack Dot.

Here they are with Mr. Dot, Mrs. Dot and Pip the dog.

This is Littletown where they all live.

There is a little blue bird to find on every page

It's market day in Littletown.

Polly and Jack like the market. Pip likes the market too.
It's busy and noisy and there's lots to see.

Mrs. Dot is by the fruit stall.

Oops! She knocks an orange with her bag.
It falls from the stall. Can you see?

The orange rolls away.

Pip thinks it's a big, bouncy ball. He wants to play.
"Come back!" shouts Jack, but Pip doesn't stop.

4

Mrs. Bird's dogs join the fun.

They jump from her arms. "Come back, Tig!
Come back, Tag!" she cries, but the dogs don't stop.

The dogs chase the runaway orange.

They pass the fish stall.

They pass the cheese stall.

They pass the candy stall...

...and run along the road.

The dogs run into Mr. Bun, the baker.

He nearly drops his tray of cakes.
"Come back!" he shouts. But the dogs don't stop.

Now more dogs join the chase.

A black
dog chases
a big dog...

...who chases
a small dog...

...who chases
a puppy...

...who chases
a spotted dog
who chases...

8

...Jack who chases...

...Polly who chases...

...Tig and Tag who chase...

...Pip, who chases the runaway orange!

9

They all run past the café.

There is a CRASH and a BANG, but the dogs don't stop.

They all race down the road.

They pass the butcher's.

They pass the post office.

They pass the bank...

...and pass the pet shop.

A boy kicks the orange.

The dogs stop! They watch the orange fly up in the air.
Polly and Jack watch it too.

12

They chase the orange back up the road.

They pass the bank.

They pass the post office.

They pass the butcher's...

...back to the market!

Pip catches the runaway orange.

He drops it at Mrs. Dot's feet. "Bad dog, Pip," she says.
"Look what you've done!"

Littletown is in a mess.

"Oh dear," says Jack. "Oh dear," says Polly.
"Oh dear," says Mrs. Dot.

"Who made this mess?" asks a policeman.

"Well, it all started with a runaway orange..." says Polly.
Can *you* remember what happened after that?